THE
PAPER WAGON

A folktale from Friesland

THE PAPER WAGON

A folktale from Friesland

Retold by
martha attema

with illustrations by
Graham Ross

ORCA BOOK PUBLISHERS

Text copyright © 2005 martha attema
Interior illustrations copyright © 2005 Graham Ross

Library and Archives Canada Cataloguing in Publication

Attema, Martha, 1949-
The paper wagon : a folktale from Friesland / retold by Martha Attema;
with illustrations by Graham Ross.
(Orca echoes)

ISBN 978-1-55143-356-1

1. Hens--Juvenile fiction. I. Ross, Graham, 1962- II. Title. III. Series.
PS8551.T74P36 2005   JC813'.54   C2004-907238-2

First Published in the United States, 2005
Library of Congress Control Number: 2004117322

Summary: When her rooster is stolen away by the fox,
the little hen builds a paper wagon and sets off to rescue him.

*Orca Book Publishers is dedicated to preserving the environment and has printed
this book on paper certified by the Forest Stewardship Council®.*

Orca Book Publishers gratefully acknowledges the support for its
publishing programs provided by the following agencies: the Government of Canada
through the Canada Book Fund and the Canada Council for the Arts, and the Province
of British Columbia through the BC Arts Council and the Book Publishing Tax Credit.

Design and layout by Lynn O'Rourke

ORCA BOOK PUBLISHERS
Box 5626, Stn. B
Victoria, BC Canada
V8R 6S4

ORCA BOOK PUBLISHERS
PO Box 468
Custer, WA USA
98240-0468

Printed and bound in Canada

14 13 12 11 • 5 4 3 2

To Femke,

whose love of books inspires me.

—m.a.

For my Mom, Marion Elizabeth

who let me wander.

—G.R.

CHAPTER ONE
The Accident

Early one morning a little hen and her rooster decided to make a big pot of soup.

The rooster built a fire underneath a black pot. The little hen filled the pot with water. She threw beets, beans, onions and potatoes into the pot.

Two wooden stools stood close to the pot. The hen and the rooster took turns stirring the soup with a big stick.

Soon a delicious smell filled the chicken coop. An aroma of cooked beets, boiled onions and tender beans tickled their beaks.

"When can we eat?" asked the rooster. "I'm hungry."

"In a little while," said the hen. "You stir the soup, and I'll get the herbs."

While the rooster stirred and stirred, the little hen ran outside to the garden. She scooted over to a sunny spot beside the coop. There she picked some parsley, a few stalks of chives and a branch of rosemary.

Back in the kitchen, she threw the herbs into the boiling soup.

"Can we eat now?" asked the rooster. "I'm starving."

"In a little while," said the little hen. "You keep stirring. I'll find some spices."

One at a time, she added some salt, some pepper and a dash of curry to the soup.

"Let's eat now!" yelled the rooster. "I'm so hungry I could faint."

"In a minute," said the little hen. "You keep stirring. I'll fetch the bowls."

While the little hen looked on the shelf, the

rooster stirred and stirred. He stood on his toes on the stool. He bent over and stirred and stirred and ... plop, fell into the pot.

"Oh, dear. Oh, dear," clucked the little hen.

She jumped onto the stool and pulled the rooster out of the boiling pot.

"Ooh! Aah!" cried the rooster.

"Oh, dear. Oh, dear," clucked the hen again. "What shall I do now?"

"Aah! I burned my feathers! Help me!"

The little hen opened the door. "You need fresh air," she said.

Grabbing the rooster by the tail feathers, she dragged him onto the front lawn. Spreading out his feathers, she said, "Lie still, and you will be dry in no time."

The rooster cried softly, but didn't move.

The little hen ran back inside to stir the soup.

Moments later she looked out the window.

A big red fox was sneaking out the front gate. The rooster dangled from his mouth.

"Oh, dear. Oh, dear," clucked the little hen. "What shall I do now?"

CHAPTER TWO
The Paper Wagon

The little hen ran to the barn beside the chicken coop. She opened the door. Sunlight streamed through the windows. Dust flew up into the air when she ran inside.

Shelves lined the walls of the barn. Two tiny harnesses hung on a hook beside the door.

"The fox's house is in the forest, but I don't know how to find it," she sobbed. "What if the rooster is injured? I can't carry him all the way from the fox's house. I need a wagon."

The little hen fetched a square sheet of white paper from a shelf. She spread out the white paper on the workbench.

"Hmm," she said. "I have an idea."

She folded the sheet of paper in half. Then she opened the paper and smoothed it flat with her wings. Holding on to one side, she folded the paper in half again. This time she folded it top to bottom. She walked on the crease and opened the paper again. The sheet of paper now had four squares. The little hen folded two sides of the sheet to the middle line. She opened the paper and folded the other two sides the same way. When she opened the sheet again it had sixteen small squares.

The little hen ran to fetch the hedge clippers. With big snips she cut off one strip of four squares. The white sheet of paper had twelve squares left.

The little hen stood back and looked at her project. She thought for a moment and cut two slits in either end of the paper. Then she went into the house to fetch the glue.

With the glue jar tucked under her wing, she ran back to the barn. The little hen brushed glue onto the four corner squares. Swiftly, she folded up the sides and the ends and stuck the sticky squares onto the sides to make a box. While the paper wagon dried, the little hen ran outside. Half flying, she scooted through the yard, looking for two sticks.

Many branches lay scattered underneath the apple tree. She picked up two that were about the same length. She noticed all the red apples lying in the grass.

"When I have my rooster back," she said, "we must gather these apples and sell them." She ran back to the barn.

Carefully, she poked two holes in each side of the wagon. The two sticks fit right through the holes.

The little hen ran outside again. "I need wheels," she panted. She remembered the vegetable garden. She found her shovel and dug up four potatoes.

"No good," she clucked. "Not round enough." She dug up four onions. Two were small and two were big. "No good," she said.

As fast as her little feet could move, she trotted over to the apple tree. There in the grass, she found four red apples.

"Perfect!" she cried. "They are all the same size." Holding two apples under each wing, the little hen ran back into the barn. She fastened one apple onto each end of the stick. Now her wagon was ready.

The little hen flapped her wings. Out of the rafters jumped two white mice.

"Hurry!" said the little hen. "We have no time to lose! We must save the rooster from the fox."

The mice stopped in front of the wagon. The little hen took the two leather harnesses from the hook. She harnessed the mice and attached the reins. She leaped onto the wagon.

"Hurry! Hurry!" she shouted.

The mice jumped into action. The little hen held onto the reins. Off drove the white paper wagon onto the road to the forest.

CHAPTER THREE
A Heavy Load

The sun shone brightly in a clear blue sky. The little hen and the two white mice had been traveling for several hours. They were just passing a turtle, when the little hen saw a tall shiny sewing needle standing at the side of the road.

The little hen pulled in the reins. "Halt! Stop!" she called.

The wagon stopped beside the needle.

"Please, Needle, can you give me directions to the fox's house? He has stolen my rooster, and if I don't find him fast, he'll eat my rooster for supper."

"I can come with you and show you how to get

into the forest. You take the path between two big, fat maple trees."

"Thank-you," answered the little hen, "but do you have time?"

"I have nowhere to go," said the shiny needle. "My master, the tailor, threw me out, because my point is too dull for sewing."

"That is not fair," said the little hen.

"I'll help you save the rooster from the fox," said the needle as it climbed onto the wagon.

"Hurry! Hurry!" cried the little hen.

As fast as their little feet could run, the mice pulled the wagon in the direction of the woods.

The road became quiet, except for two blue jays that laughed, "Jay! Jay!" when they saw the paper wagon rushing by with the hen and the needle.

At noon, they saw a hairy black spider standing at the side of the road.

The little hen pulled in the reins. "Halt! Stop!" she called.

The wagon stopped beside the spider.

"Please, Spider, could you give me directions to the fox's house? He has stolen my rooster, and if I don't find him fast, he'll eat my rooster for supper."

"I can come with you and show you how to get past the great big log that's lying on the path. You have to crawl over."

"Thank-you," answered the little hen, "but do you have time?"

"I have nowhere to go," said the hairy black spider. "A man with an enormous broom swept me out of the barn and onto the road. I'm afraid to go back."

"That is terrible," said the little hen.

"I'll help you save the rooster from the fox," said the spider as it crawled onto the wagon.

"Hurry! Hurry!" cried the little hen.

The two white mice pulled the wagon as fast as they could in the direction of the fox's house.

19

On they drove for several hours. They didn't meet anyone except for two crows that laughed, "Crow! Crow!" when they saw the paper wagon rushing by with the hen, the needle and the spider.

Later that afternoon, they saw a fat cat, standing at the side of the road.

The little hen pulled in the reins. "Halt! Stop!" she called.

The wagon stopped beside the cat.

"Please, Cat, could you give me directions to the fox's house? He has stolen my rooster, and if I don't find him fast, he'll eat my rooster for supper."

"I can come with you and show you how to get to the turn in the path to the fox's house. You have to go past the hollow tree stump."

"Thank-you," said the little hen, "but do you have time?"

"I have nowhere to go," said the fat cat with tears in her eyes. "The dear old lady I lived with had to move, and no cats were allowed in her new apartment. No siree."

"That is awful," said the little hen.

"I'll help you save the rooster from the fox," said the cat and jumped onto the wagon.

"You are far too heavy for my paper wagon!" cried the little hen.

"I'll be very careful," said the cat and sat down.

The wagon sagged to one side.

"Sit in the middle," the little hen told the fat cat.

The cat moved to the middle of the paper wagon.

"Hurry! Hurry!" cried the little hen. "We have no time to lose!"

The two white mice pulled as hard as they could, but the weight of the hen, the needle, the spider and the cat slowed the wagon down.

On they drove for several hours. They didn't meet anyone except for two ravens that laughed, "Caw! Caw!" when they saw the paper wagon rushing by with the hen, the needle, the spider and the cat.

Late in the afternoon, the paper wagon almost crashed into a big red brick. It stood in the middle of the road.

"You startled me," said the little hen as she pulled in the reins.

The wagon stopped beside the brick.

"Please, Brick, could you give me directions to the fox's house? He has stolen my rooster, and if I don't find him fast, he'll eat my rooster for supper."

"I can come with you and show you how to get to the fox's house. You have to cross the open field."

"Thank-you," answered the little hen, "but do you have time?"

"I have nowhere to go," said the big red brick. "See the ruins of that barn over there?" He pointed to a pile of rubble. "I was part of that old building. Today, some men came to break it down. One guy picked me up and threw me on the road."

"That is horrible," said the little hen.

"I'll help you save the rooster from the fox," said the red brick as it settled itself in the paper wagon.

"You are far too heavy for my paper wagon!" cried the little hen, but the red brick stayed right where it was. "Hurry! We must hurry!" cried the little hen. "We have no time to lose!"

The two white mice puffed and groaned. Their little bodies strained. They pulled as hard as they could. Slowly, the wagon wobbled along. They didn't meet anyone except for the long shadows of the trees. The trees didn't laugh, but their shadows grew darker and darker.

CHAPTER FOUR
In the Forest

As darkness fell, they entered the forest at last. They took the path between the two fat maple trees, just as the needle had said.

The wagon halted. The mice collapsed on the forest floor.

"Oh, dear. Oh, dear," clucked the little hen. "I hope we are not too late to save the rooster."

"How will we find the fox's house?" hollered the big red brick. "It is too dark to find our way. We will have to wait till morning."

"No! No!" cried the little hen. "We can't wait till the morning. The rooster will be eaten!" She paced up and down, from the paper wagon to the two white mice. "Get up! Get up!" she cried.

The two mice didn't move. They were sound asleep.

"Get off my wagon!" the little hen shouted at all the riders. "You promised to help me. If I hadn't taken you along, I would have been at the fox's house already!" She flapped her wings.

"But you didn't know the way!" they all cried.

"That is so," said the hen. "But from now on you will have to walk! We will leave the wagon here!"

One by one, the passengers climbed off the wagon.

"I'll stay with the brick," said the tall shiny sewing needle, as it stepped off the wagon. "I can't see in the dark."

"But I need your help," clucked the little hen who was close to tears. "You know the way!"

"I will help," said the fat cat. "I can see very well at night."

"I will help," said the hairy black spider.

"Okay, okay," said the needle and the brick with a big sigh. "We promised."

"Good," said the little hen. "Take me to the fox's house. Wake up, mice!" She poked the sleeping mice with her beak. Dazed and confused, they jumped up. The little hen unbuckled their harnesses.

"We have to move on until we find the great big log that's lying on the path," said the spider.

"Wait! Wait!" cried the two white mice, who were now wide-awake. "We will come with you!"

"I can see the way!" meowed the fat cat. "Let me go first!" The cat leaped up and passed the spider, the tall needle, the mice and the little hen.

"We have to stay together!" roared the big red brick. "We all promised to help save the rooster."

The little hen stopped. "That's right," she said. "The big red brick is right."

Everyone stopped. They waited for the brick to catch up.

"Let's follow the cat," said the little hen.

They all agreed. The little hen and the two mice followed the fat cat. The spider crawled behind the mice. The needle and the brick closed the line.

They stumbled along in the darkness. They didn't meet anyone except for two barn owls that laughed, "Whoo-oo! Whoo-oo!" when they saw the parade staggering through the forest, led by the fat cat.

CHAPTER FIVE
The Plan

That night clouds covered the moon.

It was hard for the small troop to stay together. Twigs and small branches scratched them. Roots and clumps of grass tripped them.

The tall shiny sewing needle had a hard time keeping up. It hopped and fell. It got stuck in the soft ground. The spider had to pull the needle out every time.

The big red brick sweated and panted. "Can we have a rest?" it gasped.

"No, no!" the little hen clucked. "We must hurry. We have no time to lose!"

Suddenly, the cat stopped. The little hen, the two white mice and the hairy black spider bumped into each other and rolled over the fat cat.

"What's the matter?" they cried as they untangled themselves from the cat. The tall shiny sewing needle and the big red brick had finally caught up with the rest of the group.

"We have found the great big log lying on the path," the cat said.

"Good," said the big hairy spider. "That means we are going in the right direction."

"But how will we get to the other side?" the little hen said. "We can't go under it. We can't go around it."

"No," said the spider. "We have to crawl over it."

The big red brick had a hard time. Everybody had to help push the brick onto the top of the log. With a crash, it fell down the other side.

"Ouch! Ooh!" the brick screamed.

The mice and the spider followed the brick over the log. The cat helped the hen. With a little help, the needle stumbled across.

With the log behind them, the little group continued on their way.

"I see the hollow stump," the cat cried out. "We have to turn right."

They followed the path to the right until the trees stopped.

"We have reached the open field!" the brick called out.

"Shhh," the fat cat hissed. "Look straight ahead." The cat pointed a paw. "There on the other side of the field, behind those pine trees, I see a tiny light. I'm sure that's the fox's house."

"Let's run for it!" the two white mice said at the same time.

"No, no!" clucked the little hen. "We have to have a plan."

"Good idea," they all agreed.

"What's the plan?" the hairy black spider asked.

They gathered around the little hen. At that moment, the clouds parted and the moon shone down on the small group.

"That helps," said the little hen. "Now we can see where we're going."

"But the fox can see us too," said the hairy spider.

"Oh, dear. Oh, dear," clucked the little hen. "What do we do now?"

"I know," said the hairy spider. "We have to sneak up to the fox's house and look in the window."

"Good thinking," said the little hen. "We have to be very quiet."

"Yes, yes." They all nodded.

"Can you be quiet?" the little hen asked the big red brick.

"I will do my best," the brick answered.

On quiet feet, the little hen, the two white mice, the fat cat and the hairy black spider continued. The tall shiny needle and the big red brick followed at a distance. Closer and closer to the fox's house they crept. No one spoke or made a sound.

A giant pine tree stood in front of the little wooden house. A yellow light shone from a small window.

"We'll wait behind this pine tree," the little hen said at last.

They all settled into the grass behind the tree. They waited.

"I'll look in the window," said the little hen. She tripped over to the house and reached the window. She stretched her neck, but she could not see inside. The little hen was too short. Defeated, she ran back to the pine tree.

"I need to make myself taller," she announced.

"No problem," said the big red brick. "I'll roll over to the window and you can stand on top of me."

"Good," said the little hen. She followed the brick to the window and climbed on top.

The window was still too high.

On soft paws, the fat cat joined them. "I'll help," she said. "I'll climb on top of the brick. You," the cat said, pointing at the little hen, "climb on top of me."

The fat cat climbed on top of the big red brick. The little hen climbed on top of the fat cat.

"We want to see too!" squealed the two white mice.

"Okay," said the little hen.

The two white mice scampered onto the little hen's back.

"Hey! What about me?" shouted the hairy black spider.

"Oh, sure! Go ahead!" the mice squeaked.

The hairy black spider crawled up the big red brick, the fat cat, the little hen and the two white mice.

"Stop tickling!" the two mice giggled.

"You forgot me!" called the tall shiny needle.

"No! No!" they all said. "We don't want you stabbing us with your sharp end."

"But I want to see!" The tall shiny needle stomped on the ground.

"Okay! Okay!" grumbled the big red brick. "You can stand on me, but you have to stand still."

"I promise," the tall shiny needle said, and with one hop landed on the big red brick.

"Do you see anything?" asked the brick.

They all looked in the window.

"I see a teacup," the hairy black spider said.

"We see a bed," the white mice said.

"I see a woodstove," the fat cat said.

"I see a chair," the needle said.

The little hen looked in the window. Her heart beat fast. Was her rooster still alive? Had they come in time to save him?

She saw the teacup and the bed and the woodstove and the chair and... "Listen," she whispered. "I hear something."

No one moved. They all listened.

A soft cockle-a-doodle wailing came from inside the fox's house.

"Quick! Let's rescue the rooster!" cried the little hen.

The mice and the hairy spider ran down the little hen. The little hen scrambled down the cat and the big red brick. The needle hopped off the brick.

"Psst. I have a plan," said the little hen. "Come here."

They all gathered around the little hen.

The little hen bent over to the needle and whispered something.

The tall shiny needle nodded.

The little hen whispered something to the spider.

The hairy black spider nodded.

The little hen whispered in the two white mice's ears.

They both nodded.

The little hen whispered something in the cat's ear.

The fat cat nodded.

The little hen bent down to whisper something to the brick.

The big red brick nodded.

CHAPTER SIX
In the Fox's House

With hope in her heart, the little hen opened the door. She looked around the fox's house. Tied to the table, with a long rope, sat her rooster. His head down, his feathers ruffled, the rooster was a sorry sight.

As soon as the rooster heard the door open, he lifted his head. He stared at the little hen. "Please, untie me. Fast!" he gasped. "The fox may come home any minute. He promised he would eat me for his supper."

The little hen ran over to the rooster. The two white mice, the tall shiny sewing needle, the hairy black spider and the big red brick followed.

"Who are they?" said the rooster.

"They are friends. They have come to help you," the little hen said proudly.

"I didn't know we had so many friends," said the rooster.

"I didn't know either," said the little hen. She turned to her friends. "Please help me untie the rooster," she said.

They all grabbed a piece of the rope. But no matter how hard they tried, they could not untie the knot. It was too tight.

"Oh, dear. Oh, dear," clucked the little hen. "What do we do now?"

The hairy black spider had crawled onto the table for a better view of the situation.

"I see something," he said.

"What is it?" they all cried.

"It's a sharp knife," the spider said.

"I'll get it," said the cat. The fat cat leaped onto the fox's table and fetched the knife. Using all her strength, the little hen managed to cut the rope.

The rooster shook his feathers. "Now, let's go home," he said. "I'm starving."

"Yes, let's go home," the little hen said.

"Wait a minute," the big red brick said. "What about the plan?"

"Yes," they all shouted. "What about the plan to teach the fox a lesson?"

"Oh, yes. Oh, dear," the little hen clucked. "I almost forgot."

"What do you mean?" the rooster crowed. "I just want to go home!"

"No, no!" they all shouted. "We have to follow our plan. Quick! Tie up the rooster! We have no time to lose before the fox comes home."

"No, no!" the rooster crowed. "That nasty fox will eat me."

"No way," said the little hen. "We're here to protect you."

The rooster's eyes were big with fear. He backed away from the table. The little hen grabbed his feathers. The big red brick blocked the door.

"Don't be a chicken," said the little hen. "Come here."

They all grabbed a piece of the rope, but before they could tie the rooster to the table they heard footsteps.

"Quick!" whispered the little hen. "Take your positions." Dragging the rooster along by his wings, she scampered to the nearest closet and hid inside.

The two white mice ran to the fox's bed and disappeared under the covers.

The tall shiny sewing needle hopped onto the fox's chair and stood on its head.

The hairy black spider crawled into the teacup.

The fat cat opened the little door of the woodstove and climbed inside.

The big red brick hobbled up the stairs to the second floor.

CHAPTER SEVEN
A Surprise Dinner for the Fox

The door opened. In walked the big red fox.

The little hen and the rooster sat in the closet, afraid to breathe.

The two white mice sat on the bed, under the covers, afraid to move.

The needle stood on the chair, still as a statue.

The hairy black spider sat in the teacup, still as a stone.

The fat cat sat inside the woodstove, quiet as a log.

The big red brick lay in a corner of the second floor, stiff as a rock.

"Aaah," the fox said, licking his lips. "It's time to make that scrumptious rooster dinner."

Then he saw the rope dangling from the table. "Nooo!" he screamed. "Where is that good-looking, juicy, fat rooster?" He looked under the table. "I will find you, rooster," he shouted. "I will find you. You are cooked!" He checked behind the chairs and under the bed. He opened the door and yelled, "Come back, you yummy rooster!"

But there was no answer. "He cut the rope," the fox gasped. "He cut the rope with my knife!" He shook his head in disbelief. "And I am so hungry," he said. Tears rolled down his cheeks.

Sad and angry, the fox sat down on his chair. "Oh! Ouch!" He jumped up and down, holding his sore behind. "That hurts! That hurts!" he cried as he pulled out the needle and threw it across the floor. The needle hopped behind the chair.

The fox ran around in circles, but after a while he calmed down. "At least I can drink my tea," he said.

He walked over to the table, picked up the teacup and took a big gulp.

"Whooph, whoa, whoomph! What's in my tea!" He choked and coughed and spat the hairy black spider across the room.

The spider crawled under the bed in a dark corner.

The fox, still coughing and shaking, walked over to the woodstove. "I'd better put some logs in the woodstove," he said. "I'm getting chilly."

He opened the stove door.

Thick clouds of ashes blew into his face and all over his shiny fur.

"Huff, splurr!" Snorting and spluttering the fox backed away from the stove. He brushed the ashes from his coat. He looked around the room. There was nobody there.

Tired and upset, the fox crawled into bed. As soon as he pulled the covers up to his chin, something tickled his paws. He tried not to think about it and pulled up his legs. He was tired, hungry, hurt and dirty. The tickling didn't stop. It got worse. It crept up his ankles, over his knees and up his legs.

The fox threw off the blankets and leaped out of bed. He jumped around the room, scratching his legs and his paws.

Before the fox could figure out what was going on, he heard a terrible noise on the second floor. He covered his ears, but the noise grew louder. By the time the brick was ready to come bouncing down the stairs, the fox had run to the door. Wailing and yelping, he ran from the house into the dark forest.

CHAPTER EIGHT
The Best Soup in the World

As soon as the little hen heard the fox leave, she opened the closet door. "He's gone!" she shouted. "He's gone!" She pulled the rooster out of the closet. The poor bird was weak from hunger and fear.

The two white mice jumped off the bed. "Did you see the fox jump and scratch?" they squeaked. They laughed so hard they had to hold their bellies.

The tall shiny sewing needle hopped around the chair. "Did you see how I pricked the fox?" The needle laughed so hard it swayed back and forth.

The hairy black spider crawled out from underneath the bed. "Did you see how the fox almost choked?" The spider laughed so hard tears ran down its little black face.

The fat cat, her fur black from ashes and soot, crept out of the woodstove. "Did you see how dirty the fox was?" The cat laughed. "Almost as dirty as me."

With loud, rumbling sounds, the big red brick tumbled down the stairs. "Did you see how the fox fled his house?" The brick roared with laughter, shaking all over.

They all laughed, until the little hen spoke. "You have done a wonderful job fooling the fox," she said. "Now it's time to leave. The fox may come back."

"I'm starving," the rooster crowed softly, and without another word he fainted.

"Oh, dear. Oh, dear," clucked the little hen. "What do we do now?"

"I'll carry him," said the fat cat.

The little hen looked at the cat. "The rooster is heavy," she said.

"I know," said the fat cat as she lifted the rooster onto her back. They all followed the cat into the dark forest.

"The rooster can lie on the wagon," the little hen said. "The mice can pull the wagon. The rest of you will have to walk."

The tall shiny needle, the hairy black spider and the big red brick looked at the little hen.

"It's too far to walk," they all said.

"You will have to," the little hen said. "You can have some soup when we get home."

The big red brick rumbled along behind the cat with the rooster, the little hen, the two white mice, the hairy black spider and the tall shiny needle.

Slowly but surely, they followed the same path they had come.

Tired and hungry, they finally found the white paper wagon where they had left it, right beside the fat maple trees.

"I need a rest," said the fat cat. She let the rooster slide off her back. The rooster opened his eyes, but was too weak to stand up.

With the help of the brick, the hen and the two mice, the cat hauled the rooster onto the paper wagon.

After a short rest, the little hen clapped her wings. "Time to go," she announced. She harnessed the mice and hopped onto the wagon.

The hairy black spider, the tall shiny needle, the fat cat and the big red brick followed.

They traveled for a while, but didn't meet anybody. The sun rose above the horizon. Birds stretched their feathers. The early morning greeted them.

After many hours they arrived at the chicken coop.

The little hen jumped off the wagon. Just at that moment the four apples came off the sticks. The paper wagon fell to the ground.

"Oh, dear. Oh, dear," clucked the hen. She ran after the apples, collected all four and gave them to the brick. "Carry these," she said. "We'll have them for dessert." She unharnessed the mice. The little hen and the fat cat helped the rooster off the wagon.

The rooster opened his eyes. "What smells so good?" he asked.

"That must be the soup," clucked the little hen. "Everyone come inside. I think the soup will be ready. It has been simmering for a day and a night."

They all sat around the small table in the chicken coop. The little hen busied herself handing out bowls of soup.

The two white mice were quiet. They feasted on the vegetable soup.

The tall shiny sewing needle dipped its head into the soup. "Where will I go?" it said with its mouth full.

"You can stay here and help me with my sewing," said the little hen.

The hairy black spider had crawled right into its bowl. They could hear it smacking. "Where will I go?" it asked.

"You can stay here and eat the mosquitoes," said the little hen.

The fat cat slurped and slurped until the bowl was empty. "Where will I go?" she asked.

"You can stay here, but..." the little hen said, looking from the cat to the white mice, "you leave those two alone, or you'll have no home."

The big red brick swallowed the soup in one gulp and burped. "Where will I go?"

"You can stay here," said the little hen. "Our window is sagging. You can hold it up."

"Thank-you," they all said.

The rooster took his time eating. As he enjoyed his soup, his feathers smoothed and his head perked up.

They all watched the rooster and waited until he was finished.

The rooster wiped his beak on the tablecloth and stood up.

"Thank-you for saving me from the fox," he said.

They all applauded.

A knock at the door stopped their clapping.

"Who could that be?" The little hen ran to the door and opened it.

Outside stood the fox. He was shivering and looking down at his feet. Big tears fell on the ground.

"I'm starving," he said in a trembling voice. "I smelled your soup from far away."

"But—" the little hen said.

"I'm sorry," said the fox, sobbing. "I'm so sorry I stole your rooster. Can I please have some soup!"

The little hen looked at his crying face.

"All right," she said. "Come in."

With eyes big with fear, they all stared at the fox.

"Oh, no," crowed the rooster.

"Sit down," said the hen, and she gave the rooster a push. "The fox wants to say something."

"I'm sorry I took you," the fox said, looking at the rooster. "But don't you think I have been punished enough?"

They all looked at the fox. They remembered the tricks they had played on him. One by one they nodded their heads.

"Can I have some soup?" the fox said softly. "I missed my dinner."

The little hen pulled up a chair. She handed the fox a bowl of soup.

He swallowed it in big gulps.

They all waited and watched.

"I never had such delicious soup," the fox said. He licked the bowl. "It's the best soup in the whole world." He looked at the little hen.

"It's my grandmother's recipe!" said the little hen.

"It's much better than my grandmother's recipe," said the fox with a red face.

"Good," said the little hen. She scratched the recipe on a card and gave it to the fox.

"Thank-you," said the fox.

The little hen, the rooster, the two white mice, the shiny needle, the hairy black spider, the fat cat and the big red brick stood in the doorway and watched as the fox walked off down the road in the direction of the forest.

martha attema has been collecting Friesian folk tales for years. She fell in love with the absurd tale of the little hen and the rooster and couldn't resist sharing it. martha lives in Powassan, Ontario, in the off-the-grid straw-bale house that she and her husband recently built.

Graham Ross created the interior illustrations for *The Paper Wagon* in pen and ink and the cover illustration in coloured inks, acrylic and coloured pencil. He lives in Merrickville, Ontario, with his family, their cat Dakota, and their dog Meka.